Nobody's Purr-fect

(Especially Not Georgie)

Angela LaCarrubba

ISBN 978-1-64416-522-5 (paperback)
ISBN 978-1-64416-524-9 (hardcover)
ISBN 978-1-64416-523-2 (digital)

Christian Faith Publishing, Inc.
832 Park Avenue
Meadville, PA 16335
www.christianfaithpublishing.com

Printed in the United States of America

For my precious gifts:
Aiden and Vincent Blondin, Kyle and Kellen
LaCarrubba, and Helene and Brandon
Sheh who "love Grandma anyway"

Acknowledgements

The creative process of writing a story and submitting it for publication is greatly improved by getting input from others. *Nobody's Purr-fect (Especially Not Georgie)* had several people who contributed to its completion and publication.

My friend, neighbor, and published author Dr. Roberta Temes provided me with collegial writing opportunities, good suggestions, and welcome support during the writing process.

Dr. Stephen Bistritz, my brother-in-law and published author, gave me input about the process of publication that was extremely helpful. He further contacted two friends who are also published authors for second opinions.

My cousin Jill Alesandro Johnson suggested that she read the story to her second-grade class to get reactions. Their responses were positive and shed light on how children view the story.

First readers and cheerleaders for the story included Claire Bistritz, Dr. Lisa LaCarrubba, Aiden and Vincent Blondin, Marc, Elaine (who found a home for Georgie in the LaCarrubba family), Kyle, and Kellen LaCarrubba, Helene and Brandon Sheh, Brian LaCarrubba and Brenda Whetstone, Brenda and Richard Brunelle, Joellen Surace, and Susan Kaplan. Their love of cats, critical responses, and frequent encouragement helped me to fine tune the story.

My literary agent at Christian Faith Publishing, Holly Dorman, who initiated the publishing process, was helpful and supportive from the start.

Allie Lasher, my publication specialist at Christian Faith Publishing, was invaluable to the process. She moved things along at a brisk pace, answered my many questions rapidly, and provided me with all I needed to turn my manuscript into a book.

My husband, Dennis LaCarrubba's, encouragement and support were constants during the entire process.

Thank you! These are small words for the big help these people provided, but the gratitude I feel is sincere, and I want to share it with them.

Preface

As you read this book, keep in mind that Georgie LoSanto is a real cat that is the inspiration for this story. He is big and mischievous. This story is based on a day when Georgie did exactly what he wanted to do, not caring how his owners would feel.

Georgie LoSanto is our family's new cat. I'm Jake, and my little brother is Todd. We are the best buddies of Georgie, our green-eyed gray cat with white markings.

Georgie is an anomaly. You say it like this, "uh-nah-ma-lee." It's a big word that Dad uses to talk about Georgie. It means he's different from many cats, but in a good way.

Here are some of the weird things Georgie does:

Georgie eats both his wet and dry cat food just like a cat does. But he also likes to eat ham.

Georgie greets people who come to our house and snakes his body around their legs, waiting to be petted.

If we hold Georgie's bowl up in the air, he stands on his hind legs begging for his food until we put his bowl on the floor. He's like a dog.

Georgie may be special, but he also can be a "big pain," as Grandma says. Georgie follows all of us when we get up in the morning by twisting around our legs. Grandma says, "One day, you'll find me on the floor because I tripped on Georgie. He's a big pain."

But Dad says, "Nobody's purr-fect, especially not Georgie. Love him anyway."

Since Grandma lives with us, I want to train Georgie so we don't find Grandma on the floor. But Grandpa only laughs when I ask him to help, and says, "That's what cats do! Nobody's purr-fect, especially not Georgie. Love him anyway."

Georgie has two scratching posts. He doesn't use them. Instead, he uses the couch. Grandma says, "Look at the scratch marks Georgie makes on the leather couch."

Georgie sharpens his claws on the leather chair in the kitchen. Grandma says, "Look at the holes Georgie puts in the chair."

Georgie climbs on the couch and sends the pillows falling to the floor like snowflakes. Grandma says, "Look at the mess Georgie makes."

Georgie scratches our bumpy wallpaper. Grandma says, "Look at the scratch marks Georgie makes on the wallpaper."

Dad says, "Nobody's purr-fect, especially not Georgie! Love him anyway."

We put a special spray on the furniture to keep Georgie away from the sofa and a different spray on his scratching posts to attract him. They don't work. We use sticky tape, a double-sided tape, to stop cats from scratching. It doesn't work. Grandma says, "Nothing but trouble, that one is. So much damage because of him."

Dad says, "Nobody's purr-fect, especially not Georgie! Love him anyway."

One Saturday, my brother and I are playing with Georgie. He chases the laser beam made by my flashlight as it moves across the floor and up the walls. He swats at his cat toy that looks like a fishing pole with a feather hanging from it. He runs from one end of the house to the other. We fall down laughing.

Later that morning, Todd and I see Georgie in the basement. "Let's play," says Todd. But Georgie doesn't move.

"What's wrong, buddy?" I ask.

Then we see Georgie's stomach go in and out. He lets out a howl and gets sick. "Something is wrong with Georgie," Todd says.

After Dad cleans up, he tells us, "There were a lot of hairballs to clean up from inside Georgie. He's getting a lot of fur in his belly when he cleans himself. We need to do a better job of brushing Georgie."

Georgie plops down on the rug and puts his head on his paws, looking up at us with his big green eyes. "Time to let Georgie rest, Todd. Let's go out to play."

We come inside after playing and look all over for Georgie. We can't find him. Dad, Grandma, Grandpa, Todd, and I look through the house in corners, boxes, and furniture— anything that looks like a hiding place. We can't find Georgie. We plop down in the family room to have a talk. Dad says, "We looked all over, up and down and inside of things, and didn't find Georgie. So we need to talk about the possibility that Georgie escaped to the outdoors."

"No!" I shout. "He just has to be inside. Outside is too bad for him. There are the cars in the street, the woods behind the house, and the wild animals that live in the woods. Then there's no fresh food or water for him. It's starting to get cold, Dad. He can't be outside. It's too dangerous for him!"

Todd just looks at me and cries, "I want Georgie!"

Dad hugs us to him and asks, "Did you boys remember to close the door behind you when you went out to play?"

I remember Dad calling after us when we went out. He said, "You know the rule, boys. Please close the door when you go outside."

"Uh-oh, Todd. We should have closed the door."

I guess saying that to a younger brother is not smart because he starts crying way more than I thought he ever could.

Dad says, "We can leave food and treats around the inside and outside of the house to attract him. Then we might be able to capture him at the same time when he comes for his food."

After the treats are all out, Dad says, "Let's go to the park, throw around the football, and climb the ropes. That might get our minds off Georgie. Grandma and Grandpa will stay here to watch for him."

But at the park, I could only think of Georgie outside in the cold, cruel world. There is a chip inside him that tells a veterinarian who he is and who owns him. But somebody would have to bring him to a vet. I can tell you, it looks bad for Georgie.

At home, we search the house again. Todd and I go upstairs to the three bedrooms with Dad's high-powered flashlight. We empty the toy box, search in drawers and closets, and flash the light under the furniture. No Georgie.

I miss Georgie so much. I call out loud to him. But the more I call and he doesn't show himself, the more I believe that he is lost forever.

Grandma and Grandpa search the first floor. They look under the furniture, in cabinets, and in the laundry room. No Georgie.

Dad tackles the basement. He looks under the stairs, in closets, on shelves, and in corners. No Georgie.

We meet in the family room. We see that Georgie's food and water have not been touched. He's gone.

I've lost my buddy, and it's my fault. *Sad* is not a big enough word to tell you how I feel.

Before bed, we send out e-mails with a picture to our neighbors to tell them Georgie is missing. We make posters of Georgie on the computer, and we post them around our neighborhood. We bring a flyer to our veterinarian in case someone brings him there.

It is 1:30 a.m. when I wake up to the sound of thunder and see lightning. *Oh no, a rainstorm! Georgie, show yourself.*

I look outside and see Dad in his raincoat with a flashlight. He is calling Georgie's name and holding up ham. *Please, please find Georgie, Dad. He's the best cat a kid could have. I love him.*

Dad walks in with his head down, and his body is soaked. When he sees me, he says, "I'm sorry, buddy, no luck."

I run to my room and cry.

Two hours later, Dad is out there again, searching and calling. Again, he comes in and says, "I'm sorry." This time, we are all awake. Dad, Todd, Grandma, Grandpa, and I hold each other in a big group hug. I turn, and Grandma is crying big, fat tears. When she catches me looking at her, she grabs me in her arms and says, "I'm so sad. Georgie is special. I don't want him to suffer."

After a restless sleep, I get up at 6:30 a.m. to search one more time in the basement—the last place I saw Georgie. It's now eighteen hours without food, water, and the litter box. I bring Dad's flashlight and head downstairs quietly so the others can sleep.

I start behind the door that is under the stairs. I move everything. No Georgie.

I go to the two old dressers. I move everything. No Georgie.

There are two bookcases in another corner of the basement. One is blue, and one is yellow. Each has four shelves. I move everything on the blue bookcase. No Georgie.

I start on the bottom of the yellow bookcase, then go to the next shelf. I move a large framed picture that doesn't go all the way back on the shelf and wonder, *What is behind it?* That's when I spot it—Georgie's bottom, with the tail coming out of a tray on the back of the shelf. I can feel my heart pounding. "Buddy, there you are! I found you! I should have stayed with you when you were so sick."

He turns his gray face toward me so I can see his big green eyes staring at me. "Oh, Georgie, I'm so happy to see you, buddy!" I put down the flashlight and scoop him up in my arms. Right away, I give him the chicken jerky treats we left for him.

When I take him upstairs to get some wet food, I yell, "I found him! I found him!"

While I put the food in the microwave for a few seconds to make it special for Georgie, Grandma walks into the kitchen and pulls me into her arms. "I'm so proud of you. You found Georgie."

Dad walks into the kitchen next. He says, "Where was he?"

"He was on the back of the shelf on the yellow bookcase, Dad."

"Jake, I'm so happy you found him." He puts up his hand to high-five me, but when I go to slap it, he grabs me and holds me tight.

"What's all this racket? A person can't sleep in this house." Grandpa is coming into the kitchen, and behind him is Todd.

When they see Georgie, Todd asks, "Where was he?"

I tell them what I told Dad. Then we all hug and pet Georgie.

Dad says, "You know what I think? Jake is the family champ today. You did what we all tried to do, but you never gave up. Three cheers for Jake!"

So that's how I found our cat, Georgie. Ever since the lost-cat episode, Grandma carries a flashlight with her when she gets up in the morning. That way, she sees him and doesn't trip. I ask her, "How do you feel about the big pain now, Grandma?"

As she watches Georgie rub his head on her shoe, she says, "Nobody's purr-fect! Especially not Georgie. Love him anyway."

Georgie

About the Author

Nobody's Purr-fect (Especially Not Georgie) is Angela LaCarrubba's first children's book. Angela is a graduate of New Jersey City University and Kean University. Her writing skills were honed at Long Ridge Writers Group in Connecticut. She and her family lived in California for six years. They returned to their New Jersey roots where Angela taught elementary school in Westfield before her retirement. Angela uses her

time these days dabbling in different things. She may be reading, writing, skiing, traveling, playing mah-jongg or pinochle, going to the gym, taking ballroom dancing with her husband, quilting blankets for her family, and spending time with her six grandchildren: Aiden, Vincent, Kyle, Kellen, Helene, and Brandon. She lives with her husband, Dennis, in Scotch Plains, New Jersey. Together they have three adult children. She can often be found in the summer poolside with her grandkids. Georgie loves to spend time with them too.

CPSIA information can be obtained
at www.ICGtesting.com
Printed in the USA
BVHW020738021019
559968BV00003B/9/P